MARTHA SPEAKS

Farm Dog Martha

Adaptation by Karen Barss
Based on a TV series teleplay written by Peter K. Hirsch
Based on the characters created by Susan Meddaugh

HOUGHTON MIFFLIN HARCOURT
Boston • New York • 2009

Green Light Readers and its logo are trademarks of Houghton Mifflin Harcourt Publishing Company.

For information about permission to reproduce selections from this book, write to Permissions, Houghton Mifflin Harcourt Publishing Company, 215 Park Avenue South, New York, New York 10003.

Library of Congress Cataloging-in-Publication data is on file.

ISBN: 978-0-547-21060-5

Design by Stephanie Cooper

www.hmhbooks.com
www.marthathetalkingdog.com

Manufactured in China
LEO 10 9 8 7 6 5 4 3 2 1

Martha is going to a farm for the first time.
The farm belongs to a man named C.K.
"I'm going to love the farm," Martha
says. "I think."

Martha asks, "Can I do some farm chores?"
"Sure! We herd the sheep, feed the
chickens, and milk the cows," says C.K.
Martha cannot wait to begin in the morning.
Those chores sound like fun.

It is late when they arrive.
Wooo-rooo!
"What is that sound?" asks Martha.
C.K. tells her not to be afraid.

"A hound dog lives next door," C.K. says.
Martha wonders.
Dog howls are not so scary.

The next morning C.K.
wakes Martha.
He says, "Rise and shine."
"But it is still dark out!"
Martha cries.
C.K. says farm chores begin
before the sun rises.

Here is their task:
First, they will herd the sheep.
The sheep must be moved from
the pen into the pasture.

C.K. tells Martha that the sheep
are stubborn.
But Martha tells the sheep what to do.
The sheep go out the gate!
No problem.

"Good job, Martha," C.K. says.
"Now you keep the sheep in the pasture.
I will milk the cows."
C.K. leaves Martha alone with the sheep.

Martha talks to the sheep.
"Eat as much as you want.
But stay in the pasture."
The sheep walk into
the woods.

"Baaaaa!" say the sheep.
They say the woods are part
of the pasture.
Martha believes them.
She goes to see what other
jobs she can do.

Martha enters the hen house.
"Any chores for me here?" Martha asks.
The hens say, "Cluck!"
"You want me to sit on your eggs?"
Martha asks.

No problem.

Martha sits.

"Oooh, nice and toasty," Martha says.

She sees a photo on the floor.

What a mean-looking dog, she thinks.

cluck

Soon C.K. goes into the house.
He finds a surprise.
Sheep and chickens
are everywhere.
This is a problem.
"The chickens belong in the
hen house."

"And the sheep belong in
the pasture," C.K. says.
"The pasture is the grassy
area where they can eat."
"They tricked me!"
says Martha.

Late that night, Martha
hears the sheep.
*They are trying to trick me
again,* she thinks.
But the sheep sound scared.
Martha runs to the pasture.

Martha sees a mean-looking
dog in the pen.
The sheep are trapped!

Martha opens the gate for the sheep.
But Martha gets locked in the pen!
The mean-looking dog comes closer.
It is a coyote!

Martha is brave.
She barks.
She growls.
The coyote runs away.
The sheep are safe.

"Thank you for saving the sheep," C.K. says. "You are a great farm dog, Martha."
Martha beams.
"It was no problem!"

Martha thinks farm chores are fun. Would you like to work on a farm? Your first task is to put the animals back where they belong.

chore   herd   pasture   rise   task

Did you notice all these new vocabulary words? Are you unsure of their meanings? Look for clues in the text to help you understand what they mean.

Unscramble these words.
Then use them to finish the sentences.

RHED   TEARSPU   AKST   EIRS   ERHCO

Rise and shine!

Martha learned how to _herd_ the sheep.

Milking the cows is a farm _chore_ .

The sheep spend their time in the _pasture_.

Sitting on eggs is a _task_ for chickens.